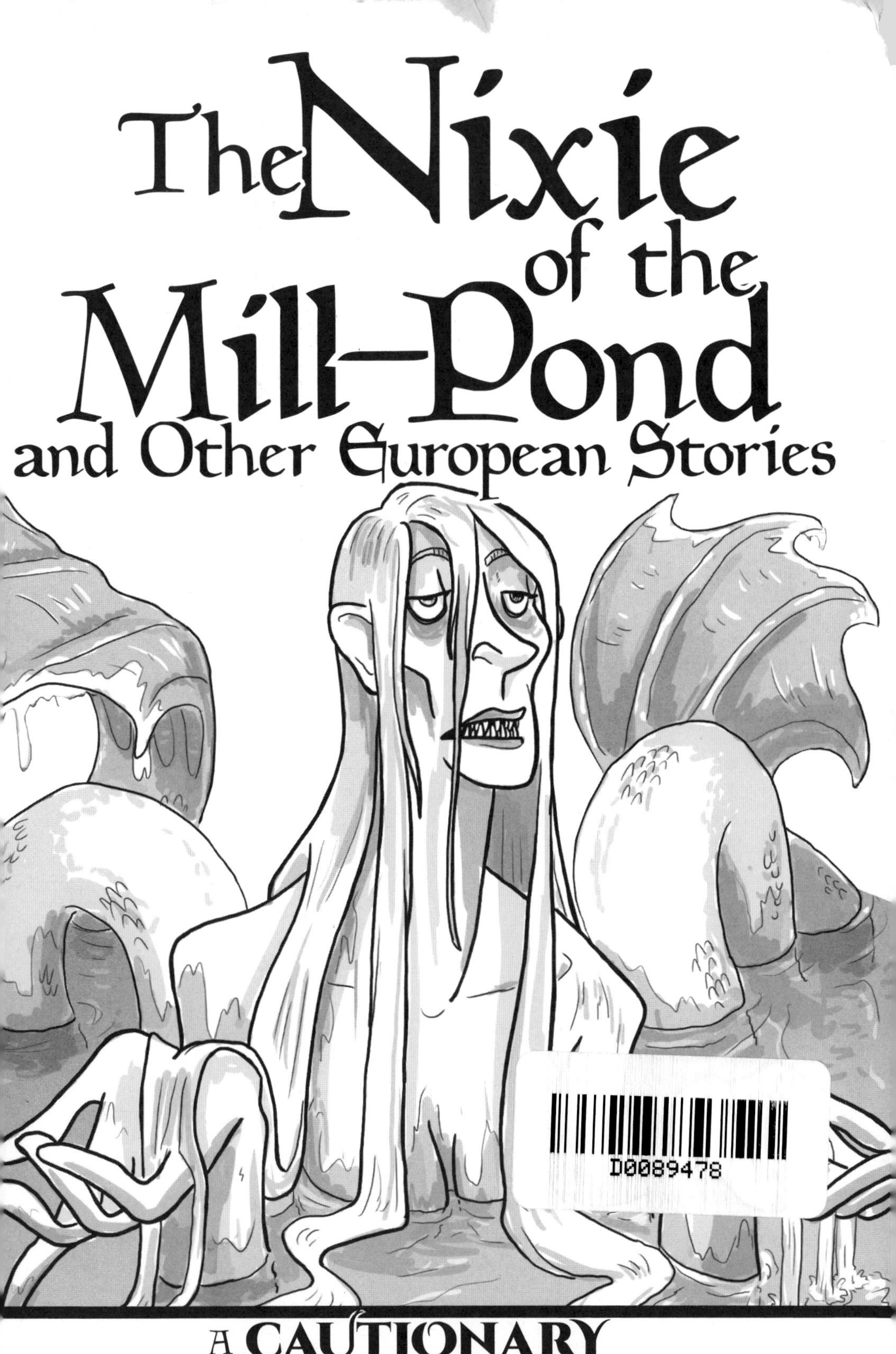
The Nixie of the Mill-Pond
and Other European Stories
A CAUTIONARY
FABLES & FAIRYTALES Book

editors
Kel McDonald & Kate Ashwin

publisher
C. Spike Trotman

art director & cover design
Matt Sheridan

proofreader
Abby Lehrke

print technician & book design
Beth Scorzato

published by
Iron Circus Comics
329 West 18th Street, Suite 604
Chicago, IL 60616
ironcircus.com

first edition: April 2020

print book ISBN: 978-1-945820-54-0

10 9 8 7 6 5 4 3 2 1

Printed in China

inquiry@ironcircus.com
www.ironcircus.com

strange and amazing

CAUTIONARY
FABLES & FAIRYTALES

Also Available:

The Girl Who Married a Skull and Other African Stories

Tamamo the Fox Maiden and Other Asian Stories

The Nixie of the Mill-Pond and Other European Stories

Publisher's Cataloging-In-Publication Data
(Prepared by The Donohue Group, Inc.)

Names: McDonald, Kel, editor, author. | Ashwin, Kate, editor, author. | Spike, 1978- publisher. | Sheridan, Matt 1978- designer. | Scorzato, Beth, designer.
Title: The Nixie of the mill-pond, and other European stories / editors, Kel McDonald & Kate Ashwin ; publisher, C. Spike Trotman ; book designers, Matt Sheridan, Beth Scorzato ; proofreader, Abby Lehrke ; print technician, Beth Scorzato.
Other Titles: Cautionary fables & fairytales (Series) ; 3.
Description: First edition. | Chicago, IL : Iron Circus Comics, 2020. | Interest age level: 008-012. | Summary: "Explores some of Europe's most famous fables and lesser known favorites, from sly humor to dark fireside tales and everything in between"--Provided by publisher.
Identifiers: ISBN 9781945820540
Subjects: LCSH: Fairy tales--Europe--Comic books, strips, etc. | Europeans--Folklore--Comic books, strips, etc. | CYAC: Fairy tales--Europe--Cartoons and comics. | Europeans--Folklore--Cartoons and comics. | LCGFT: Fables. | Fairy tales. | Graphic novels.
Classification: LCC PZ7.7 .N59 2020 | DDC [Fic] 398.2094--dc23

Table of Contents

DUCE
COME ON, AT LEAST TRY TO LOOK PRESENTABLE.
IF SOMEONE DOESN'T BUY YOU, MOM'S GONNA BE SO MAD.
PLUS, Y'KNOW, THE WHOLE PENNILESS STARVING THING.
MY, WHAT A FINE COW!
!
Y-YA REALLY THINK SO?
OF COURSE!

YES, LOTS OF FINE EXPERIENCES IN THIS OLD GIRL.
Y' DON'T SAY?
HOW MUCH ARE YOU ASKING FOR HER?
UH...
WHATCHA GOT?
HAHA,
WELL LET'S TAKE A LOOK HERE.
I THINK I MIGHT HAVE SOMETHING OF PARTICULAR USE TO YOU.
?
HERE WE ARE.
??
...JUST BEANS?
HAHA, OF COURSE NOT *JUST* BEANS.
???

OBVIOUSLY THEY'RE NOT JUST BEANS!
I WAS INFORMED THAT THESE HERE ARE MAGICAL BEANS!
YOU TRADED... OUR LAST COW... FOR THESE...
YOU ARE...
CRUNCH
THE WORST SON...
EVER!
CRAUNCH
BUT MA!!
GO TO BED, RIGHT NOW!
AND NO SUPPER TONIGHT!
AND HOPE THAT THERE WILL BE SUPPER FOR TOMORROW.

JACK and the BEANSTALK
AS ADAPTED BY MARY CAGLE

GRUMBLE
UGH...
WHAT TIME IS IT?
IT DOESN'T SEEM *THAT* SUNNY YE-
WHAT THE *WHAT!?*

I TOLD HER THEY WERE MAGIC!
IT'S ALMOST LIKE...
STAIRS?

HUFF
HUFF
IS THIS... THE TOP...?
...WHOA.
THAT'S... UNEXPECTED.

H-...
HELLO?
...THIS PLACE SURE IS BIG.
...UH...
EH?
WHAT A BEAUTIFUL SONG...
IS SOMEONE THERE?

KREAAAAAAK
WHY, IT'S JUST A HUMAN BOY!
HOW DID YA GET HERE, LITTLE FELLA?
B-BUH-BEANSTALK, MA'AM.
WELL ISN'T THAT SOMETHIN'!
COME ON IN, I'M JUST FINISHIN' DINNER.
NO NEED TO BE SHY!
I WON'T EAT YA!

FEE! FIE! FOE! FUM!
UH OH.
WELL HE'S HERE EARLY.
YOU'LL WANT TO BE HIDING, THEN.
W-WHY? WHO'S HE?
JUST MY HUSBAND, BACK FOR DINNER.
WHY DO I NEED TO HIDE THEN?
BECAUSE HIS FAVORITE DINNER IS HUMAN.
SLAM
I SMELL THE BLOOD OF AN ENGLISHMAN!

OH HONEY, YOU ALWAYS THINK YOU SMELL ENGLISH MEN.
IT'S PROBABLY JUST THE LEFT-OVERS.
HRMPH! IF YOU SAY SO.
PHEW
IS MY DINNER READY?
IT WILL BE IN A MOMENT.
DID YOU POLISH MY TREASURE LIKE I TOLD YOU TO?
TREASURE?!
$ $
YES DEAR, FIVE TIMES TODAY, AS ORDERED.
I SURE COULD USE SOME TREASURE...
OR SOME FOOD...
GRUMBLE
DID YOU HEAR SOMETHING?!
NOW WHAT ARE YOU GOIN' ON ABOUT?
...HRMN.

HM?
OH NO! GREAT PLACE TO DOZE OFF, ME!
I GUESS THEY'RE GONE...?
CREAAAKK
STILL CURIOUS ABOUT THAT MUSIC...

...WAS IT COMING FROM HERE?
HRNNGGG!
CREAAAAK
WHOA NELLY!

G-GOLDEN EGGS?
DON'T MIND IF I DO...
THAT'LL SHOW MISTER GIANT PEOPLE EATER.

HM?
IS THAT WHAT WAS MAKING THE MUSIC?
BUT THEN WHO WAS PLAYING IT?
YOINK.
WHO ARE YOU SUPPOSED TO BE?

YOU CAN TALK!?
WHAT'S IT LOOK LIKE, YOU LITTLE THIEF!?
HEY, I'M NOT A THIEF!
THEN WHAT DO YOU HAVE ON YOUR WAIST THERE?
ER...
SOUVENIRS?
THIEF IN THE TREASURE ROOM!

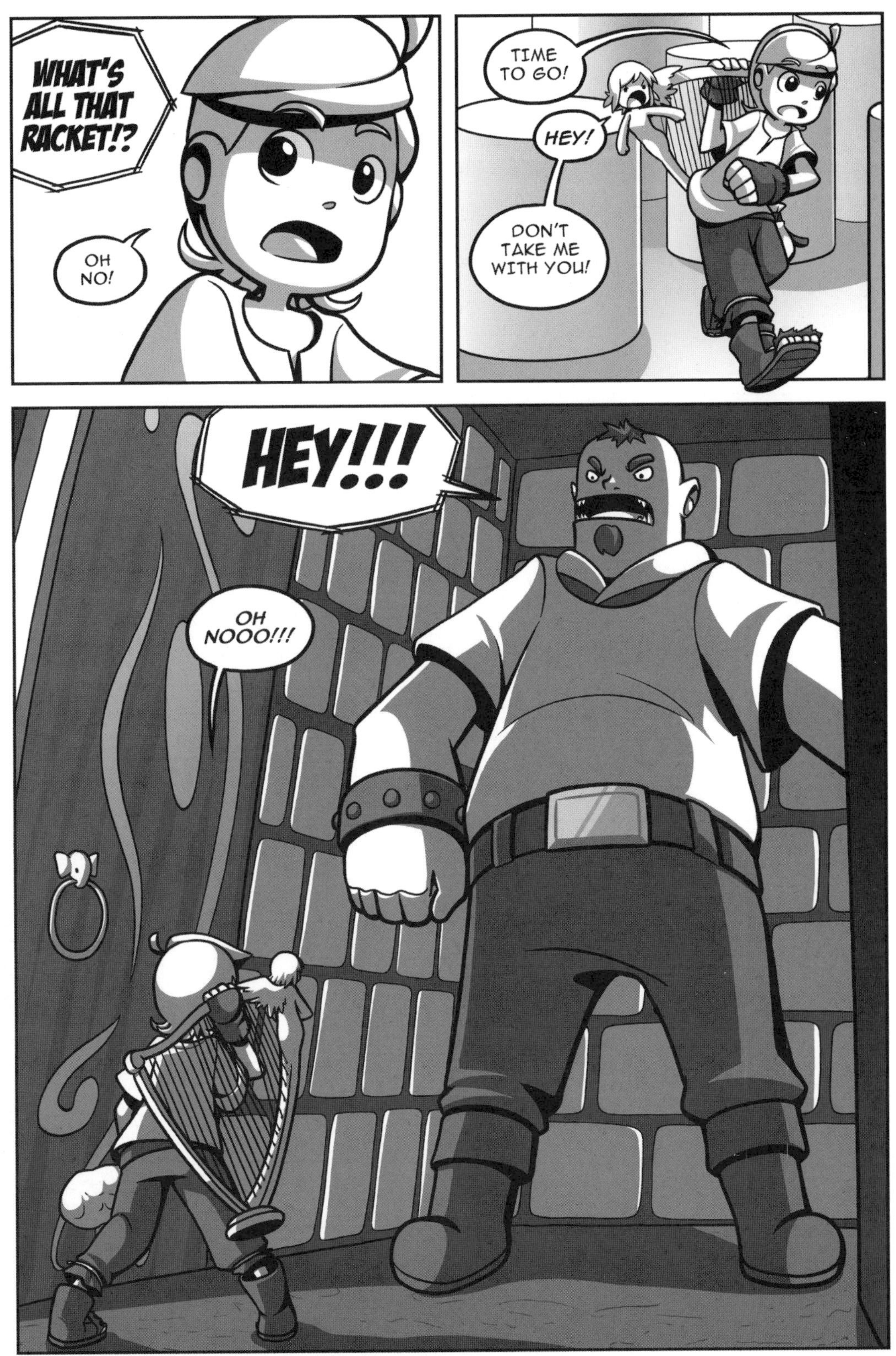
WHAT'S ALL THAT RACKET!?
OH NO!
TIME TO GO!
HEY!
DON'T TAKE ME WITH YOU!
HEY!!!
OH NOOO!!!

COME BACK HERE, YOU LITTLE RUNT!
YOU'RE IN FOR IT NOW, KID!

WHY ARE YOU TAKING ME ANYWAY?
I WANTED TO ASK YOU SOMETHING!
ME?
ARE YOU THE ONE WHO WAS PLAYING THAT REALLY PRETTY MUSIC EARLIER?
YOU CAN'T GET AWAY, LITTLE HUMAN!
I'LL GRIND YOUR BONES TO MAKE MY BREAD!
Y-YOU THOUGHT IT WAS PRETTY?
HUFF THE PRETTIEST MUSIC I'VE EVER *HUFF* HEARD!

...MASTER ALWAYS SAYS THAT MY MUSIC SOUNDS REALLY STUPID.
I DON'T MIND THAT SO MUCH.
HE ALSO *HUFF* Y'KNOW, *HUFF* WANTS TO EAT ME?
CASUAL PACE!
END OF THE LINE, BOY!
HUFF THAT'S WHAT YOU THIN-
WHOA!

DOOF
OH BOY.
OW
OW
OW
OW
OW
OW
OW
HATEMYLIFE.
WHO PUT THIS THING HERE!?

JACK!
MOM!
WHAT IS THAT THING!?
WHAT ARE YOU DOING UP THERE!?
I'M COMING DOWN!
WAIT THERE!
B-BE CAREFUL!
YOU AREN'T GETTING AWAY WITH MY TREASURE!

GROOOOOAAAAAAN
...WHAT.
HURRY, KID! THE STALK IS LEANING!
YOU'RE KIDDING ME!

CRAASH
...WHAT A LAME WAY TO GO.
WHAT EXACTLY HAPPENED UP THERE, JACK?
I'LL TELL YA THE WHOLE THING LATER.
BUT FIRST, CAN WE PLEAAAASE GO GET SOME FOOD?
I'D LOVE TO, IF WE HAD ANYTHING TO BUY FOOD WITH.
OH, DON'T WORRY ABOUT THAT!
I'M SURE SOMEONE WILL ACCEPT GOLD.

UM..,
NOT TO INTERRUPT THIS WHOLE FAMILY REUNION THING...
BUT DO DO YOU THINK OTHER HUMANS WOULD LIKE MY SINGING?
YOU'RE A MAGICAL TALKING HARP!
I'M SURE PEOPLE WOULD PAY TO HEAR YOU SING EVEN IF...
YOU SUCKED... AT... IT...
$INFINITE MONEY COMBO!$
OH MY GOD, I'M A GENIUS!

TONIGHT
ONE NIGHT ONLY
THE ACT THAT'S BEEN SWEEPING THE NATION!
JACK AND THE SINGING HARP!
LISTEN TO THE HARP'S BEAUTIFUL MELODIES!
HEAR THE HEROIC TALE OF HOW THIS YOUNG BOY SAVED THE MAGICAL HARP FROM A FAMILY OF FEROCIOUS GIANTS!
YOU LITERALLY WON'T BELIEVE YOUR EYES!
THE END

THE SINGING BONE
by
KC GREEN

WANTED
WILD BOAR
WRECKING
HAVOC
THIS BOAR HAS RIPPED THROUGH MANY A MAN AND WOMAN AND CONTINUES ITS CARNAGE.
IF NO ONE CAN STOP IT, OUR VILLAGE IS DOOMED!
THAT IS WHY, AS KING OF THE FOREST, I OFFER A REWARD...

YOU WOULD RECEIVE MY DAUGHTER'S HAND IN MARRIAGE...
AND A LIFETIME SUPPLY OF... OF CARROTS. SURE, WHY NOT.
CARROTS?!
ANYTHING! JUST GET RID OF THAT WILD BOAR!

SLAP
A LIFETIME SUPPLY OF CARROTS?!

A GIRLFRIEND!
A WIFE!
A WIFE?
TO KISS??

I GOTTA GET THAT REWARD!

YOU CAN'T SHARE... A WIFE.
NOR CAN YOU A LIFETIME CARROT SUPPLY.

dash!

THEY WERE WRONG ABOUT BOTH OF THOSE THINGS. STILL, OUR TWO HEROES EACH SET OFF...
...TO SLAY THE WILD BOAR AND CLAIM THE PRIZES FOR THEMSELVES.

BUT...
FOREST
BAR
WELL, MAYBE A QUICK ONE...
IT IS NEVER A QUICK ONE, THAT IS WHAT ALCOHOLICS SAY.
FOREST
BAR

ANYWAY
I SHOULD HAVE BROUGHT...
...ANYTHING.

OH, I DID NOT THINK THIS THROUGH...

YAAAAAA
TAKE.
THIS.

THIS.
YAAAA
TAKE THIS LANCE AND FEARLESSLY ATTACK THE BOAR WITH IT.
AND YOU WILL KILL IT.

AND THAT
IS WHAT
HAPP-
ENED

WHAAAAAAT

FOREST
BAR

HA!
HA HA
AAAAAAA
Y-Y-Y

Y-Y-Y-Y-Y-Y-
YOU DID IT!
YOU DID IT AND YOU DESERVE A DRINK!
ON ME! C'MON!

TELL ME HOW YOU PULLED IT OFF.
FOREST
BAR
WELL...
HOURS LATER...
HA HAHAHA HA HA HA

I HAVE TO ADMIT!
YOU DID WELL, FRIEND!
NO ONE DESERVES THAT REWARD MORE THAN YOU...
EXCEPT
ME!

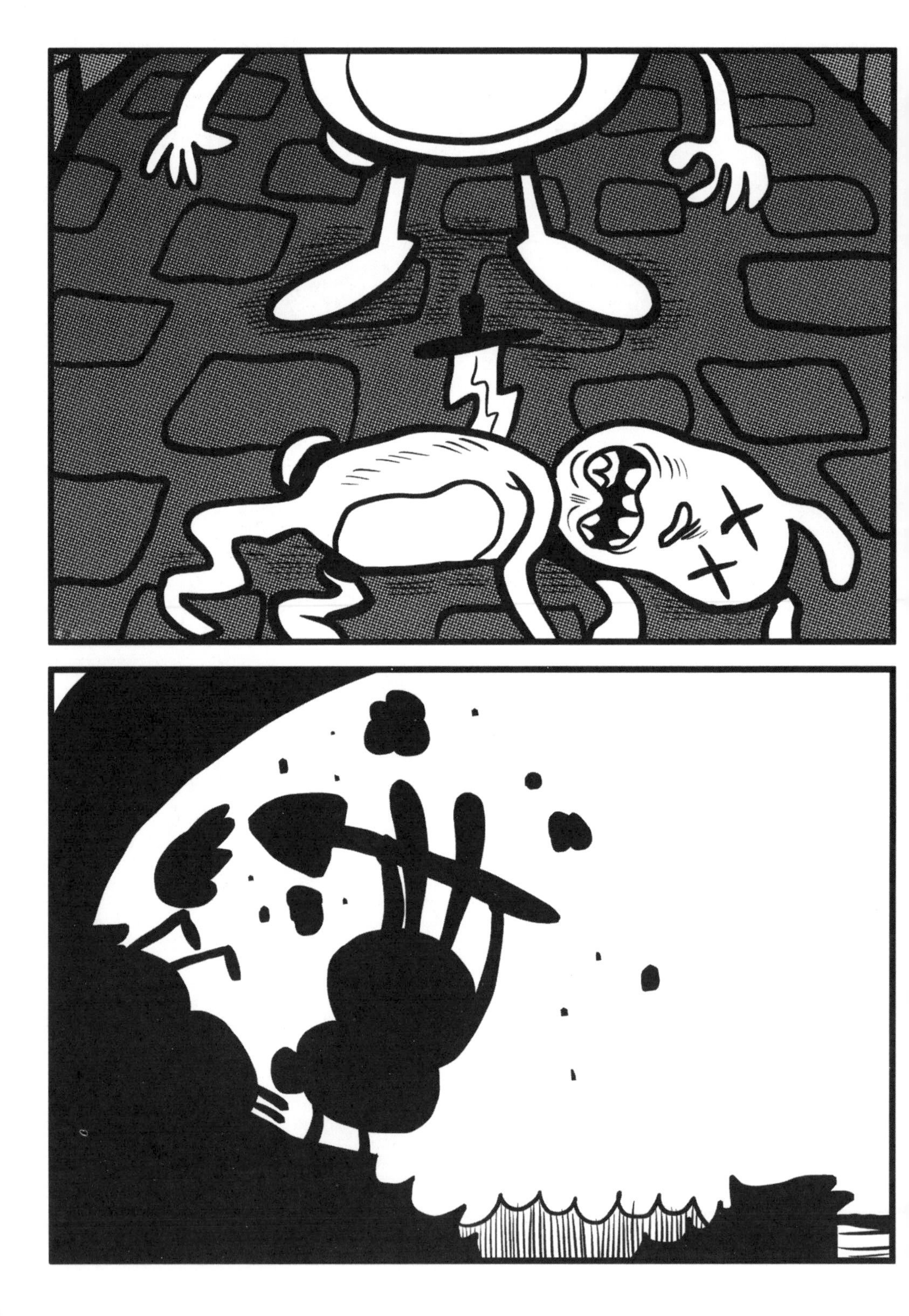

AND UNDER THE BRIDGE, HIS BODY WILL STAY.
MMMY REWARD.

drag

MANY YEARS PASS...

TOOT!
TOOT
TOOT
TOOT

OH DEAR SHEPHERD~
YOU ARE BLOWING ON MY BONE~ MY FRIEND STRUCK ME DEAD~ THE FAT, SHORT RABBIT~
AND BURIED ME BENEATH THE BRIDGE~
TO GET THE WILD BOAR FOR THE DAUGHTER OF THE KING~

AND THAT LIFETIME CARROT BUSINESS, TOO ~
dash!

SO...
THE DAUGHTER OF THE BLAH BLAH
~AND THE LIFETIME CARROTS ETC. ETC.

UH.
OH
WHATEVER

dig!
SHOVE
TOOT!
TOOT!
TOOT TOOT

the end.

Puss in Boots
by Kate Ashwin
SONS.. MY DEAR SONS.
I AM DYING, MY SONS.
FATHER, NO!
IT CAN'T BE TRUE!
SURELY NOT BEFORE YOU'VE FINISHED YOUR WILL!
AN OLD MAN KNOWS WHEN HIS TIME IS DONE. GATHER ROUND, MY CHILDREN, AND LISTEN WELL..
TO YOU, MY ELDEST, I LEAVE THE MILL, MY GREATEST TRIUMPH.
TO YOU, MY SECOND, I LEAVE THE MULE OF THE MILL. HE WILL SERVE YOU WELL.
..OH. WELL THAT'S.. *NICE*, I GUESS.
AND TO YOU, MY YOUNGEST..
ER..
?
ARE WE DONE? CAN I GO BACK TO MILLING NOW?
..*THE CAT*. YOU CAN HAVE THE CAT.
I BELIEVE YOU MAY NEED HIM..

AND SO IT CAME TO PASS THAT THE OLD MAN DID INDEED DIE, AND HIS SONS WENT THEIR SEPARATE WAYS WITH THEIR INHERITANCE.
ugh.
B-BUT I DON'T WANT TO GO! I WANT TO MILL! IT'S ALL I KNOW HOW TO DO!
NOT A CHANCE, YOU'LL BE AFTER FIFTY PERCENT NEXT!
slam!
AND TAKE YOUR MOG WITH YOU!
mrow!
BUT.. BUT.. HOW CAN I MILL WITHOUT A MILL..
A MILL, YOU SAY?
WHAT A COINCIDENCE!
IT JUST SO HAPPENS THAT MILL ACQUISITION IS MY SPECIALITY!

BUT YOU'RE A *CAT!* HOW CAN YOU GET ME A MILL?
HOW DO YOU THINK YOUR FATHER GOT HIS IN THE FIRST PLACE?
I-
TRUST ME, DEAR BOY! ALL I NEED IS ONE SMALL FAVOUR FIRST.
PERRRFECT!
THAT WAS ALL OF MY SAVINGS..
ALL OF MY MILL MONEY..
SPENT ON CAT BOOTS..
MILL THIS, MILL THAT.. YOU MUST LEARN TO THINK *BIGGER!* ***RICHER!*** NOW WAIT HERE, MY LITTLE MEALTICKET.
BUT-!
?
TO THE KING FROM THE MARQUIS CARABAS
ONE DAY:
?
THE NEXT DAY:
AND THE DAY AFTER:

I DON'T UNDERSTAND, THE KING CAN'T MILL..
IF THIS WORKS, YOU MAY BUY A THOUSAND MILLS!
NOW GO WASH YOURSELF IN THE RIVER, THE PRINCESS IS ON HER WAY!
I DON'T WANT A PRINCESS.. JUST A-
MILL, RIGHT, YES! IT IS A MEANS TO AN END!
CLEAN UP QUICKLY, WILL YOU, SHE WON'T CARE FOR THAT RATHER SHEEP-LIKE AROMA.. I KNOW I DON'T!
THAT'S RIGHT, TIDY UP NICELY..
..FOR TODAY, YOU MEET THE LOVE OF YOUR LIFE!

AH-HEM HEM.. MEOW! I SAY, MEOW!
WHAT IS THIS? A CAT?
MEE AND INDEED, OW! YOUR HIGHNESS!
WHAT A FINE LITTLE CAT YOU ARE!
YOUR HIGHNESS IS TOO KIND! I AM BUT THE SERVANT OF A MARQUIS.
CATS AREN'T MEANT TO WEAR SHOES.
A SERVANT OF A LORD SHOULD ALWAYS BE WELL TURNED OUT, DEAR.
OH GREAT, A WEIRDO THAT PUTS CLOTHES ON HIS PETS. CAN WE GO?

UH.. I SWORE I HAD SOME CLOTHES BEFORE..
PUSS? PUUUSSSS?
PUSSss...
WOULD THAT BE THE CAT I SAW STEALING YOUR CLOTHES, GOOD SIR?
I DO BEG YOUR PARDON, BUT I WAS WANDERING IN THE WOODS AND YOU LOOKED LIKE YOU COULD USE SOME HELP..
UH..
I AM BUT A SIMPLE MILLER, BUT I TRY TO HELP OTHERS WHEN I CAN.
UH..
M-MILLING? YOU'RE A MILLER? YOU HAVE A MILL?
WHY YES, IT'S PRACTICALLY ALL I KNOW! I LOVE TO MILL!
..MARRY ME.
haha!

OH LITTLE LOOORD..!
YOU'RE A LORD?! I DIDN'T MEAN TO PRESUME, AH-
W-WAIT..!
TIME FOR YOU TO PLAY YOUR PART, MARQUIS!
COME ALONG, OUR CARRIAGE AWAITS!
BUT-!
I PRESENT YOUR HIGHNESS WITH THE GREAT MARQUIS DE CARABAS!
CARABAS, CARABAS.. SOUNDS FAMILIAR.
THE DEAD BIRD GUY.
AH YES, THE ONE WHO'S BEEN PRESENTING US WITH SUCH FINE GAME!
MY LORD IS IN A FIX, YOUR HIGHNESS! BANDITS HAVE STOLEN HIS CLOTHING WHILE HE BATHED IN THE RIVER!
AN OUTRAGE! MARQUIS, PLEASE SHARE OUR COACH, I'M SURE WE CAN TAKE YOU BACK TO YOUR ESTATE!
THAT'S GREAT, DAD, GIVE A LIFT TO EVERY NAKED STRANGER WE MEET. CAN'T SEE THAT EVER GOING WRONG.

SO, MARQUIS.. IS THERE A MRS DE CARABAS YET..?
GAWD, DAAAAD!
A WHO OF WHAT-?
AH-HEH, NO, NOT AS YET, SIRE, MY MASTER IS SO VERY SELECTIVE!
SELECTIVE..
YES, THAT SOUNDS VERY FAMILIAR.
OH DAD..!
HE LIKES ANIMALS! YOU LIKE ANIMALS!
WELL.. YOUR CAT IS SORT OF ADORABLE, EVEN WITH HIS LITTLE BOOTS ON..
MY LADY FLATTERS ME!
Prrrrr
HUH? MM, CATS ARE.. YEAH, NICE..
TELL ME OF YOUR ESTATE, MARQUIS, HOW FAR AWAY IS IT?
prrrrrruh-oh.

AH, I MUST GO AHEAD AND PREPARE THE ESTATE FOR YOUR HIGHNESS' VISIT!
OH, YOU NEEDN'T-
SHAN'T BE LONG!
ESTATE, ESTATE, ESTATE..
AH-HAH!
YOU THERE! THE KING'S COACH IS COMING ALONG THIS WAY! AS HE GOES PAST, BE SURE TO BOW TO YOUR MASTER, THE MARQUIS DE CARABAS!
?
THE WHO?
MARQUIS DE- LOOK, IT'S VERY IMPORTANT TO THE KING, SEE? AND IF YOU DON'T, WELL..
..YOU KNOW WHAT HAPPENS WHEN KINGS GET UPSET, DONT YOU?
GULP!
GHK!
R-RIGHT! YES! MARQUIS! LOVE THE GUY!

The Marquis is coming!
You Must bow to him!
...or WHO KNOWS what will happen?!
ONE LAST THING.. THAT CASTLE THERE, WHOSE IS IT?
THE OGRE CASTLE, SIR CAT?
..OGRE CASTLE. AM I TO ASSUME THAT IS NOT JUST A CHARMING NICKNAME?
AN OGRE LIVES THERE!
MARVELOUS.
A TERRIBLE SHAPESHIFTER OF A BEAST! YOU MUST STAY AWAY, LEST HE EAT YOU UP!
SHAPESHIFTER, EH..
I DO BELIEVE I HAVE AN IDEA..

HMM..
THE WINDOWS PERHAPS? OR AN UNLOCKED DOOR?
NO, FAR BETTER..!
DEAR OGRE! FANCY A SPOT OF TEA?
Knock
Knock
..AND THEN THE KING SAYS TO ME, "WHICH WAY IS THE ESTATE?". SO I JUMPED OUT OF THE WINDOW.
HAW HAW HAW!
A SHAME, REALLY, THAT HE'S THE HUMAN AND YOU'RE THE CAT, YOU'D MAKE A BETTER GO OF IT!
I RATHER AGREE! SO YOU SEE, IF WE CAN JUST BORROW YOUR CASTLE FOR A LITTLE WHILE-
YOU COULD, YOU COULD..
BUT YOU SEE, I'M HUNGRY..
..AN' CAT'S MY FAVORITE SNACK!

WHILE IT'S ALWAYS NICE TO BE THE FAVORITE, I MUST DECLINE.
YOU DON'T GET TO-
YOU SEE, I CANNOT POSSIBLY BE EATEN BY A LIAR.
A LIAR?!
I HEARD TELL YOU WERE A SHAPESHIFTER. SUCH NONSENSE!
I AM TOO!
PROVE IT! BECOME.. AN ELEPHANT!
BZAP!
THERE! SEE?
HMM, NOT BAD! TRY.. A GIRAFFE!
ZA-POW!
LOOK!
WELL, YOU KNOW, THEY'RE SO BIG, *OF COURSE* YOU CAN BE THOSE.. BUT I IMAGINE YOU CANT BE SOMETHING LIKE ***A MOUSE***..
EASY! NOW STAND STILL WHILE I-
-EAT.. YOU..
gulp!

NOT BAD! RATHER ZINGY, ACTUALLY!
RMM
NOW WHAT IS-?
BBBLLL
OH MY!
HOW VERY-
-DIFFERENT!
WELL NOW.. THIS RATHER CHANGES THINGS..

SO.. MARQUIS.. WHAT SORT OF ..MUSIC DO YOU LIKE?
HUH?
S'gh
MARQUIS! DEAR MARQUIS!
I HAVE A CHANGE OF CLOTHES FOR YOU! PLEASE, YOUR MAJESTY, IF YOU WOULD ALLOW?
WHATEVER.
DAAAAD..
NEVER JUDGE A MAN UNTIL YOU'VE SEEN HIM IN HIS FINERY, MY DEAR!
UNLESS THERE'S A SPARE PERSONALITY IN THERE, I DONT SEE IT HELPING!
SLIGHT CHANGE OF PLAN!
WHAT?
BUGGER OFF.
REALLY? CAN I?
GO AND RUN FREE, LITTLE ONE! HAVE YOUR MILLS OR WHATEVER!
YES! YES I WILL!

IF I MAY RETURN, PRINCESS?
OH GREAT, WHY COULDNT HE HAVE JUST GOT LOST IN THE-
..WOODS..
FAIR LADY! APOLOGIES FOR MY PREVIOUS BEHAVIOUR!
THAT'S, UH, OK.. I.. ER..
I WAS SO DISTRAUGHT TO BE IN SUCH DISARRAY AROUND BEAUTY AS RADIANT AS YOURS!
ALLOW ME TO INVITE YOU BOTH TO MY HUMBLE ESTATES.
WE GRACIOUSLY ACCEPT, MARQUIS!
FINERY! YOU WERE SO RIGHT!
BUT OF COURSE! YOU DON'T BECOME KING WITHOUT BEING SO VERY WISE, MY DEAR!

AND SO IT CAME TO PASS THAT THE ONCE PUSS IN BOOTS BECAME THE PRINCE IN BOOTS.
HE AND THE PRINCESS HAD A LONG, HAPPY MARRIAGE..
..THOUGH SHE DID WONDER WHY SHE WAS MOVED TO SCRATCH HIM BEHIND THE EARS AT TIMES.
Just married
The End

Once upon a time, there was a quiet kingdom.
the reason for this, believed the queen, was that there were no children running about.
siiigh
no pitter-patter of feet, no giggles nor tears. just silence.
the queen would bring this to her husband's attention every day, until he finally suggested...
Siiiiigh
GO GRAB SOME KIDS FROM THE NEIGHBORS. THEY PROBABLY HAVE A FEW EXTRA RUNNING ABOUT.
-hmph
and so, the queen went to visit the neighbors.
tup tup tup
GOOD AFTERNOON, PEASANT.
OH, HELLO THERE DELORIS!
NOW WHAT BRINGS Y'ALL THE WAY OVER HERE?
pssh
SNAP
I REQUIRE CHILDREN. HAND THEM OVER.
WELL I'D JUST LOVE TO OBLIGE, BUT THESE HERE LI'L RASCALS AREN'T FOR SALE.
hee hee
giggle hee hee
YE-GADS WOMAN...
JUST HOW DID YOU COME ABOUT SUCH PLENTIFUL OFFSPRING?

THIS BUNCH HERE? WELL I HAPPEN TO HAVE THE SUPER SECRET METHOD OF BEARING BABIES.'
... YOU HAVE MY ATTENTION.
WELL M'AM, WHATCHU WANNA DO IS...
"WASH YOURSELF WITH TWO BUCKETS O' WATER."
"THEN POUR THAT THERE BACK-WASH UNDER YOUR BED BEFORE YOU GO TO SLEEP."
SPLASH
"THE NEXT MORNING, TWO FLOWERS WILL BLOOM."
"A GORGEOUS LI'L FELLER..."
"AND THE UGLIEST FLORAL TO EVER FANDANGO."
YOU WANNA EAT THE PRETTY ONE, 'N BEFORE YOU KNOW IT, YOU'LL HAVE YERSELF A LI'L BUN IN THE OVEN.
tug tug
WHAP
WHAP
WHAP
AND YOU CLAIM THIS METHOD IS SOUND?
AS SOUND AS SOUP...
ZIP!
BUT WORD OF ADVICE...

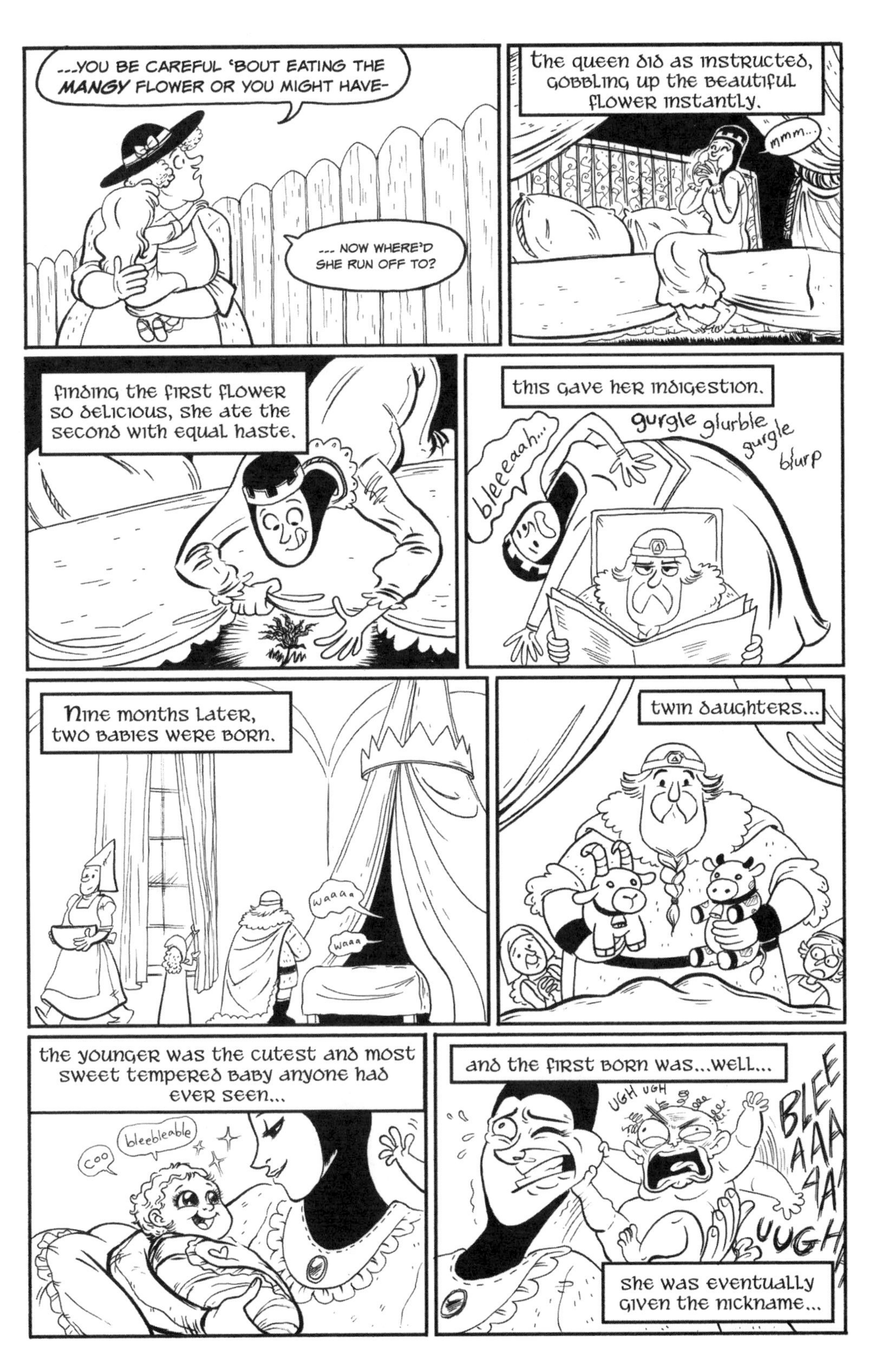

...YOU BE CAREFUL 'BOUT EATING THE MANGY FLOWER OR YOU MIGHT HAVE-
--- NOW WHERE'D SHE RUN OFF TO?
the queen did as instructed, gobbling up the beautiful flower instantly.
mmm...
finding the first flower so delicious, she ate the second with equal haste.
this gave her indigestion.
bleeeaah...
gurgle glurble gurgle blurp
Nine months later, two babies were born.
waaaa
waaa
twin daughters...
the younger was the cutest and most sweet tempered baby anyone had ever seen...
coo
bleebleable
and the first born was...well...
UGH UGH
BLEE AAA 4A UUGH
she was eventually given the nickname...

TATTERHOOD
adapted by shaggy shanahan
drawn by katie shanahan
the twins couldn't be any more different. where one was the perfect model for all things sweet and lovely...
Sniffle
Sniff
the other was unkempt, unruly, disobedient and couldn't sit still.
bleeeeh
and they were the best of friends.
A few years later, on christmas eve...
CRASH!
they heard such a clatter.

T-T-TROLL RUSH!!!
STOMP
STOMP
TROLL RUSH!!!
WHAT'S GOING ON, MUM?
YOU WERE TOO YOUNG TO REMEMBER THE LAST ONE, BUT EVERY SEVEN YEARS ON CHRISTMAS EVE WE HAVE A TROLL RUSH IN THE CASTLE.
OH, THEY TRASH THE PLACE ALRIGHT, BUT IT'S BEST TO LET THEM DO AS THEY PLEASE.
HOPEFULLY THEY'LL LEAVE SOONER THAN LATER.
TROOOOLLSSSSAAAAAA
But as the evening went on, the trolls continued to make a mess of the castle.
KICK
SHAKE
SHATTER
tink
CRACK
TINKLE

SHAKE
SHAKE
chew
chew
chew
SPLAT
FLICK
until tatterhood...
had...
enough.
THAT'S IT!!
SPLAT
LEAP!
YOINK
OUT!!

OUT!
OUT!
OUT!
bleeeh!
baaah
IT'S HIGH TIME SOMEONE DROVE THESE TROLLS BACK FROM WHENCE THEY CAME!
NO TATTER, YOU MUSTN'T!
THEY ARE FAR TOO DANGEROUS!
DON'T WORRY, LITTLE SIS.
TATTER'S GONNA SAVE CHRISTMAS.
... IT'S NOT CHRISTMAS I'M WORRIED ABOUT.
LOCK THE DOORS! AND NO ONE IS TO COME OUT, NO MATTER WHAT YOU HEAR!
SLAM
HUMPHREY?
bleeegh
grumble grrr
grumble
grr
LET'S RIDE.

the sounds of a grand battle seeped through the walls and floor, filling the castle with more crashes and booms than had been heard before.
BIFF!
ZING
GET BACK HERE!
CLINK
CRACKLE
SMACK
BOOM
ZING
CRASH
BANG
BWAHAHA!
ON GUARD!
tinkle
THUNK
HONK
ding
CRUNCH
BAM
BAM
THUD THUD THUD
THUNK
OHO!
BAM
TAKE THAT!
SMASH
tink
tinkle
But they quickly grew quieter.
...
TATTER?
CREEEEEE
EEEEEEEEEEAAAAAAAAH!
BANG
TUM TUM TUM TUM TUM

UNHAND ME YOU-
HEY!
POP
GASP!
BONK
AAAAAH! HELP ME TATTER!
HEEEEELP!
CRASH
tink tink
MOO?

meanwhile...
THE DAY IS WON!
WAVE
STOMP
STOMP
LOOK FAMILY! I DROVE AWAY THE INVADERS AND-
clip clop cl
YEE-GADS!?
BOO MOO MOOO
tatterhood scolded the entire castle for not protecting her only sister...
YOU ALL SUCK!!
PAT PAT
and set off straight away for the trolls' hideout to reclaim her sister's lost head.

It wasn't long before they arrived at troll island, where the trolls secretly lived.
STEALTH IS THE KEY HUMPHREY.
the troll village was dark and quiet, all but for one house full of trollish festivity and cheer.
BOOM
CHA
BOOM
HOO HA HA
BWA HA HA HA!
RAAA!
HO HO
BAM
THUNK
GET IN-
GET OUT-
NO ONE'S THE WISER.
gossip

CHA
CHA
BOOM
BOOM
BOOM
GAHA HAHA!
DUM DUM
BOOM
BWAHA
CLAP
CLAP
CLAP
CLAP
BWAAAA
CLAP
CLAP
CLAP
WOOO!
CLAP
CLAP
SNAP

GIANT WOODEN SPOON
WHAM
BIFF
NOOOOOOOOOO!
CHOMP
botf
Biff
BANG
MOOO
CRACK

And what a brawl is was. tatterhood spooned out swift justice upon all her foes!
PAFF
BONK
BIFF
THERE YOU GO. TOLD YOU I WAS GONNA GET YOUR HEAD BACK.
WELL, I TOLD YOUR BODY ANYWAY.
CREEE
OH TATTER...
RAAAHR!
EEEECK
CRACK
UM...I HAVE TO ADMIT...
THIS IS THE WEIRDEST CHRISTMAS I'VE EVER HAD!
YEEEEEHAW! TO THE BOAT, HUMPHREY!
SNAP

SEE YOU IN SEVEN YEARS, CHUMPS!
FLOOM
CRACK
MOO
tatterhood and crew sailed through the night on the route home...
but then came a change in plan.
SAY, WE'VE NEVER ACTUALLY BEEN AWAY FROM HOME BEFORE HAVE WE?
WHAT SAY YOU AND I KEEP SAILING...
SEE THE WORLD.
THAT SOUNDS FANTASTIC, SIS...
BUUUUT...
... COULD YOU SWITCH OUR HEADS BACK FIRST?
OH! RIGHT.
tap tap
and so...

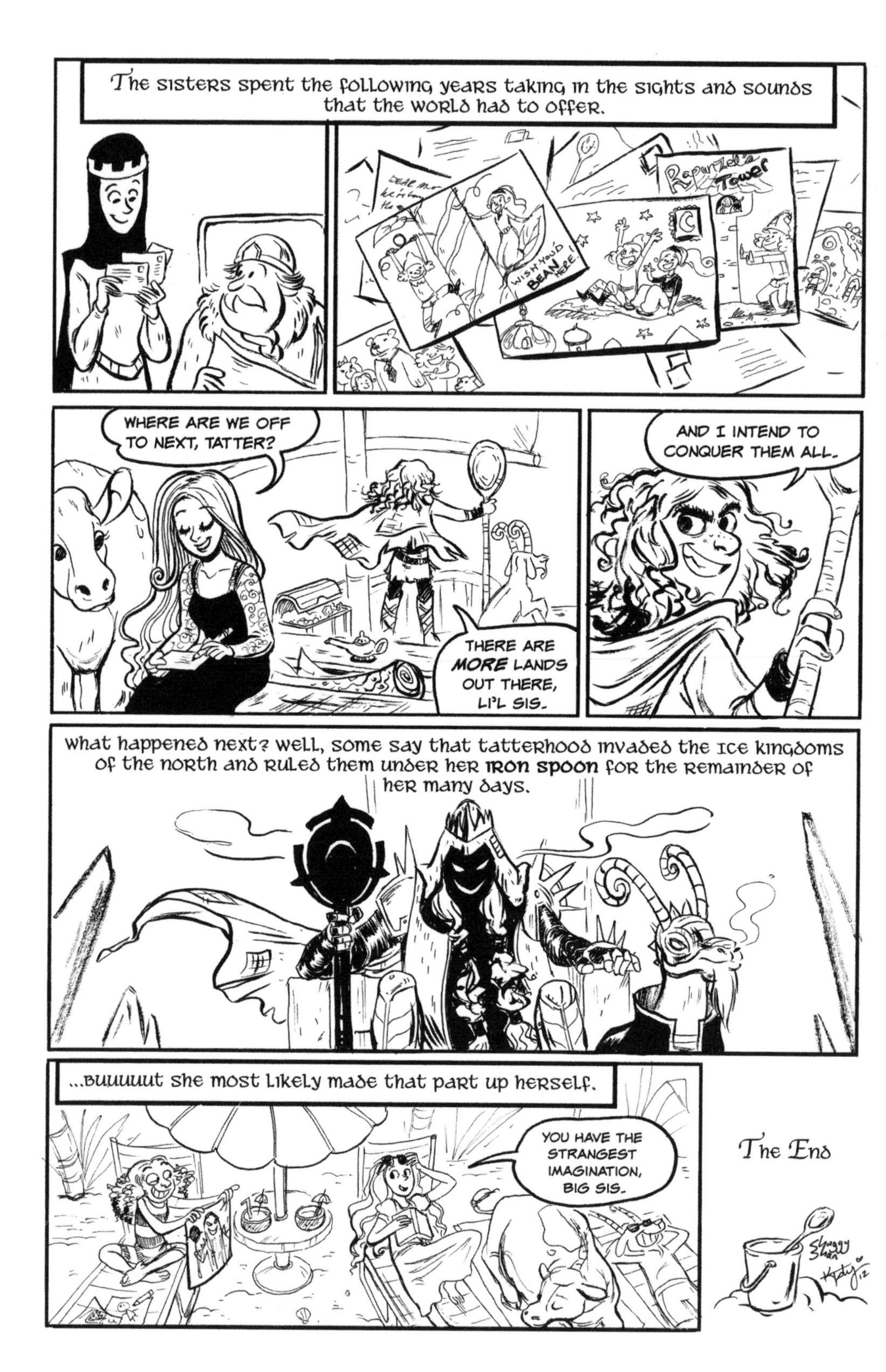
The sisters spent the following years taking in the sights and sounds that the world had to offer.
Rapunzel's Tower
WISH YOU'D BEAN HERE!
WHERE ARE WE OFF TO NEXT, TATTER?
THERE ARE MORE LANDS OUT THERE, LI'L SIS.
AND I INTEND TO CONQUER THEM ALL.
what happened next? well, some say that tatterhood invaded the ice kingdoms of the north and ruled them under her iron spoon for the remainder of her many days.
...buuuuut she most likely made that part up herself.
YOU HAVE THE STRANGEST IMAGINATION, BIG SIS.
The End

Rapunzel
by Ovens

Phew, How does that witch climb up here every day? Her Strength must be immense.
Not to mention the Weight forced upon your head...
Please forgive me for causing you pain fair maiden. I am Prince Rupert of Castle Bastock.

What is the matter Fair maiden?
Puh...
Please don't eat me...
HAHA, What lies that witch has woven into your pretty head!?
I am Just a mere man. I would never 'eat' or cause harm to you.
Now don't be afraid and rise.
I promise you shall be safe near me at all times.
Muh- Mother tells tales of men! They are horrible, foul tales. You are nowhere near what I pictured a man to be...

HAAHHAHAA
What a life you live. To be trapped in this tower and fed only lies!
AHH!
...
you have a bone stuck...
That's not a bone it's an adam's apple.
What is it for?

I'm not quite sure actually...
In my castle there are thousands of books that have answers to questions just like this.
Not to mention all the other things you are missing out on, being trapped in this tower all day!
It does sound really nice...
COME with me!
You want to see the outside right?
I bet you have never seen a horse before! You will be amazed by the amount of things you are...
No, please stop...
I can not leave the premises of this tower.

Prince...
I am bound to this castle in many ways. I can not just up and leave on a whim one day... There's a...
If it's your hair, we can cut it off and use it as a ladder to get down the tower!
Certainly not! I would die if my hair is cut!
This witch has a tighter grasp upon you than I may know...
I will try to show you what you are missing out on, maiden.
Please, permit me to visit you again.
Yes. Now hurry, mother will be home soon

A Relationship began to blossom between maiden and man.
The Prince Visited almost every day. He would often bring Rapunzel flowers that reminded him of her beautiful hair.
The relationship Started to become Something...
More...
Untill one morning.
Rapunzel...

Phew.
Rapunzel?
So you are the wretch that has been visiting my child every time I leave...
UNHAND HER!!
I will slay you witch!
Foolish boy.

FOUL Wench! you Keep Rapunzel Stashed away here in this tower!
All by HERSELF!
You have ruined the purity of my once beautiful daughter.
TAKE YOUR CLAWS OFF HER!
I Will Set Rapunzel free!!

It's only HAIR!
WAKE UP!

Foolish boy.
You indeed have set Rapunzel free. She and your unborn child have left this world. You stole her from me, and now I steal from you.
AAAAAAAAH!
Rapunzel...

'12
Ovens

Once there lived two children named Alyenushka and Ivanushka.
NO, YOU CAN'T DRINK FROM A DIRTY PUDDLE ON THE ROAD.
BUT I'M SO THIRSTY...
WE'LL COME TO A PROPER WELL SOON.
BUT PUDDLES. YOU JUST DON'T DO THAT.
They were children of the road, Alyenushka and her
"Kid Brother"
a Russian Folk Tale retold by Carla Speed McNeil
YOU SAY THAT, BUT YOU NEVER SAY WHY NOT.
FOR-THE HUNDREDTH-TIME, BABY...
ALL THE WATER IN THE WOODS IS--
MEHH.

There were, of course, good reasons.
EHH...?
I-IVANUSHKA??
OH NO!
WHY COULDN'T YOU WAIT?? OH, YOU SPOILED, STUBBORN LITTLE--
NNGH
OH MAMA I'M SORRY
I DIDN'T KEEP HIM SAFE
MAA-AA-AAA!
A wealthy man happened by, and asked Alenushka her trouble.
Upon hearing her name, he declared that their two fathers had been loyal brothers-in-arms in the last war.

Bogdan Ilych (for that was his name) offered Alyenushka a place at his table — as his wife.
THERE'S JUST ONE THING...
OOH, HERE IT COMES... KILL A DRAGON? SOLVE A RIDDLE? LAKE OF FIRE?
hnnngh!
mehhh.
ADOPT HER GOAT?? YESSS!
So Bogdan Ilych swore to keep Ivanushka as his own, and give him the best of everything.
But on the morning of the wedding, Alyenushka found Ivanushka gone.
IVANUSHKA

BABA TOOK HIM.
"BABA" ...?
OUR STOCK-KEEPER?
BABA'S THE BEST-- SHE'S WHY WE EAT SO WELL?
SO WHERE. DID "BABA". TAKE MY GOAT?
uhmm
uh-- I ah-- T-TO PASTURE? THE LAKE?
I-I DON'T KNOW! BABA DOESN'T ANSWER QUESTIONS!
MAAA!
MAAA!
MAA!

NO!
KUNCHH
TT!

AFTER HIM!
FLY!
HARD NOPE.
UH HUH NAH.
STINGY OL' BAT.
YEAH, SOD OFF, GRANNY.
HA HA HA

Here Bogdan Ilych's troubles multiplied. His beloved bride-to-be grew pale and nervous, took no food, struck her maids, slept in fits, then told of nightmares so terrible they made one sick to hear.
And she blamed it all on Ivanushka.
BUT YOU MADE ME SWEAR TO PROTECT HIM! "LIKE A CHILD," YOU SAID!
HE STINKS.
GOATS ARE GOATS--
HE HAUNTS ME. HE HAS AN EVIL SPIRIT ABOUT HIM.
I JUST DON'T UNDERSTAND... YOU LOVED THAT BEAST SO MUCH...
NO MORE.
TRUE LOVE DIES EVERY DAY.
FINE!
YOU KILL HIM! I'LL HAVE NO MORE TO DO WITH IT!

MAAA!
FLAPP
MAAAAAA
AAAAAAaaaa...

AAAA!
AAAAA!
Baby brother
I can't save you
the water has me
the stones and serpents
they HOLD me
Iva
nussh
Iva
nussh
Kaa

AAAA!
AAAA!
HUFF KOFF
SO, BOGDAN ILYCH.
YOU HAVE YOUR BRIDE.

I HAVE MY PAY.
m-maa
FIVE GENERATIONS OF YOUR FAMILY HAVE PAID ME FOR MY GIFTS.
LAND, FINE STEEL, LIVE BIRTH, THE OCCASIONAL FLYING STOVE.
YOUR DEAR PAPA BOUGHT YOU A BRIDE. A LOVE MATCH.
SO WE'RE SQUARE.
But you CHEATED, Baba.
You didn't GIVE him his bride.
You gave me to the WATER.
But... the water gave ME some things.
FLIK!
GNAAH!

HAUUGHH
NOW we're square.
Still want to marry me?
I DO, BUT NOW, UM... I SUPPOSE WE WON'T HAVE KIDS.
Maybe... maybe not.
Either way...
FLIK!
ehhh!
...We still have IVANUSHKA.
The End!
yaaa!

The Nixie of the Mill-pond
collected by the Brothers Grimm
adapted by Kory Bing
Once upon a time there was a Miller.

He lived contentedly with his wife.
They had money and land.
Their prosperity increased from year to ye
But misfortune comes overnight.
And soon the Miller scarcely owned
the mill where he lived.

He was in great distress. When he lay down after a day's work, he found no rest, but tossed and turned in bed, filled with worries.

One morning he got up before day break and went outside, thinking the fresh air would lighten his heart.

Old Miller...

Old Miller...
Why are you so sad?

At first the Miller was speechless.

...he took heart and told her how he had lived with good fortune and wealth, but now he was so poor he did not know what to do.

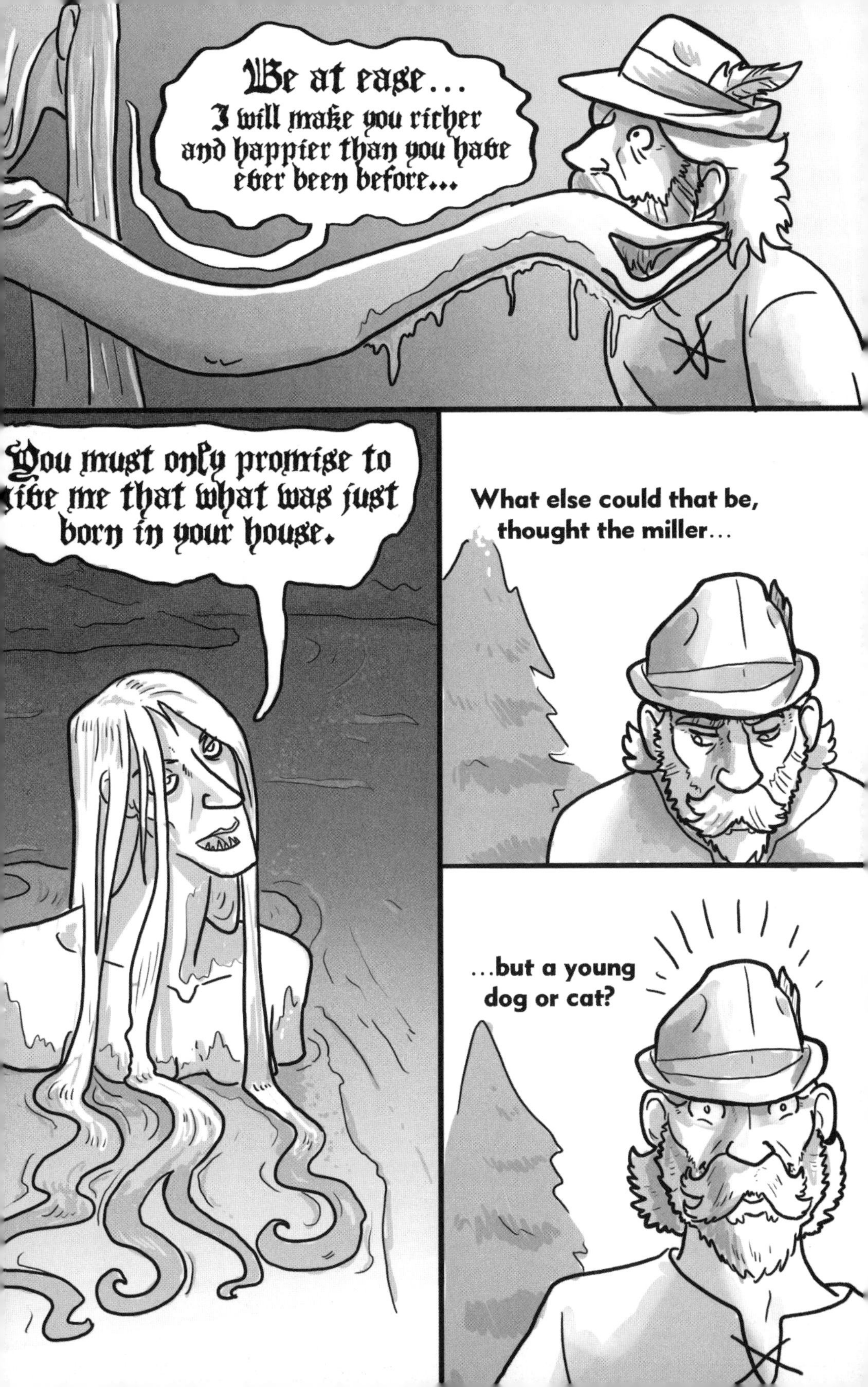
Be at ease...
I will make you richer and happier than you have ever been before...
You must only promise to give me that what was just born in your house.
What else could that be, thought the miller...
...but a young dog or cat?

So he promised her what she demanded...
...and the Nixie descended silently into the water
Consoled and in good spirits
he hurried back to his mill.
He had not yet arrived there when a friend of his wife came to the front door.

She told him to rejoice!

For his wife had just given birth to a little boy.

With a lowered head, the Miller sadly explained to his wife the promise he had given the Nixie.

"What good to me is fortune and prosperity...

...if I am to lose my child?"

The Nixie was true to her word.
Good fortune returned to the Miller's house.
He succeeded in everything he undertook.
Before long his wealth was greater than it had ever been.
However, it did not bring him happiness,
for his agreement with the Nixie tortured his heart.

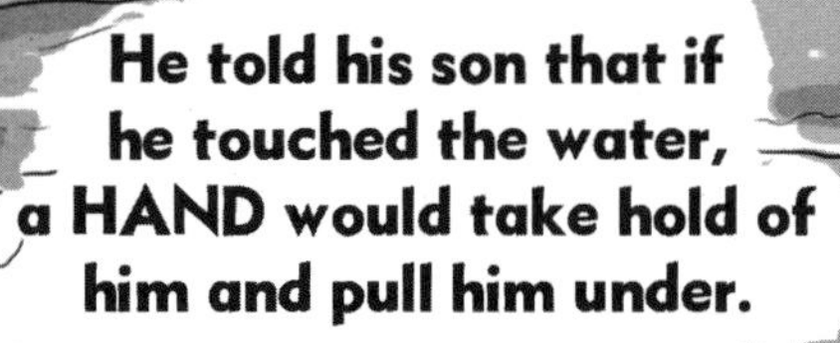
Whenever he passed the pond, he feared she might demand payment.
He never let his son go near the water.
He told his son that if he touched the water, a HAND would take hold of him and pull him under.
However, year after year passed, and the Nixie never appeared.

The boy grew...
...into a young man.
In time, he had become a skilled huntsman, employed by the lord of a nearby village.

The huntsman was well-known and much loved.
In the village there lived a beautiful and faithful maiden whom the hunstman liked, and she liked him in return.
They were soon married, and the two lived happily and loved each other.

One day the huntsman was pursuing a deer.

CRACK

Old Miller's son.
Old Miller's son. My payment is due.

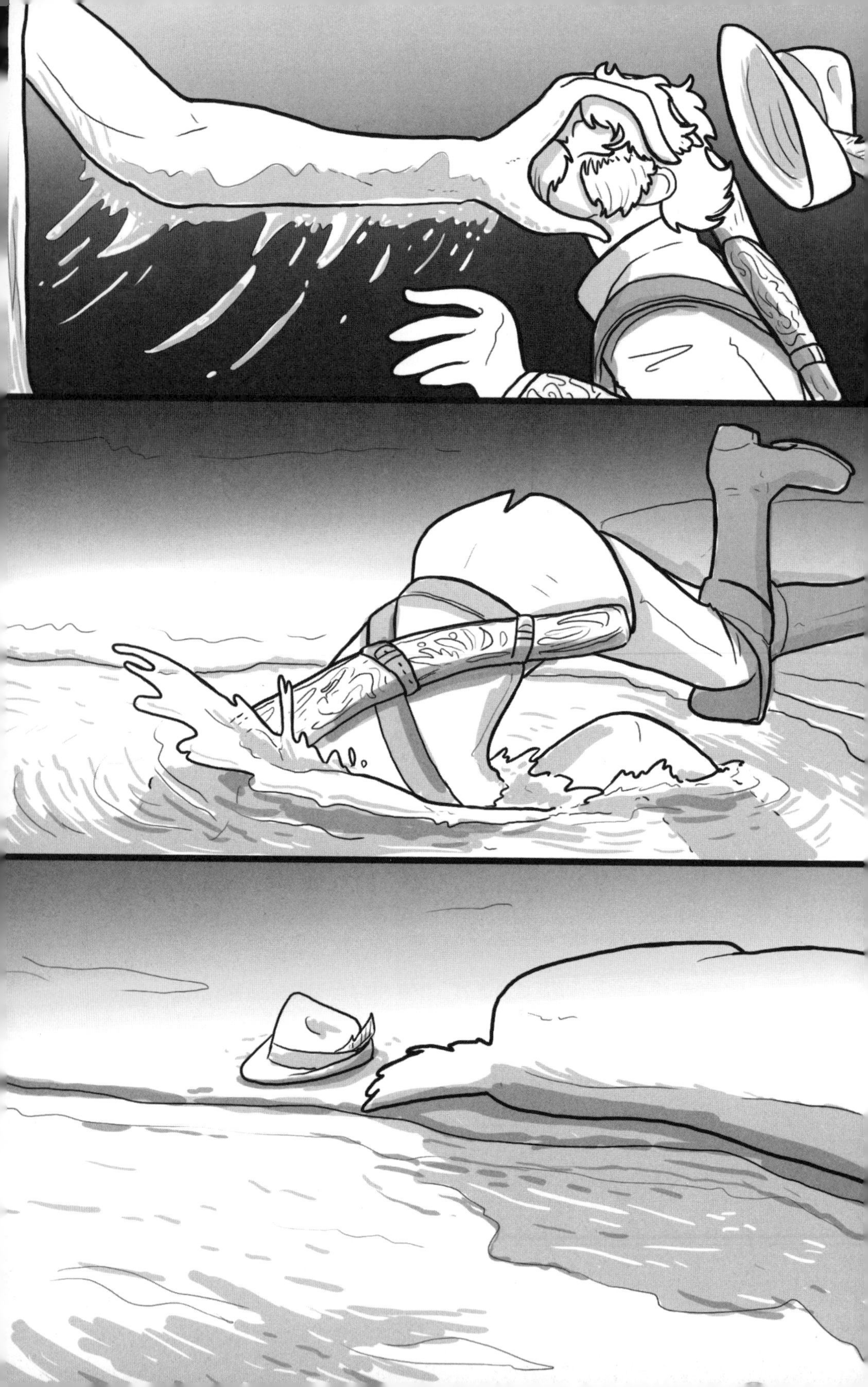

When it was evening and the huntsman did not return home, his wife became frightened and went out in search of him.

After hours of sobbing and calling his name, she collapsed.

And soon she was in a deep sleep.

Soon she was immersed in a dream.
She was fearfully climbing upwards. Rain was beating her in the face. The wind billowed her hair about.

When she reached the top, the sky was blue.
A soft breeze was blowing.
A green meadow replaced the rocky cliff.
An old woman in a small cabin called to her.

And then the poor woman awoke.
But she followed her dream—
and found the cottage
and the old woman.

You must have met with misfortune, having sought out my lonely cottage.
The woman related with tears what had happened to her.
Be comforted. I will help you.

Take this flute.
Wait until the full moon rises, sit at the bank and play a beautiful tune.
“Then you will see what happens.”

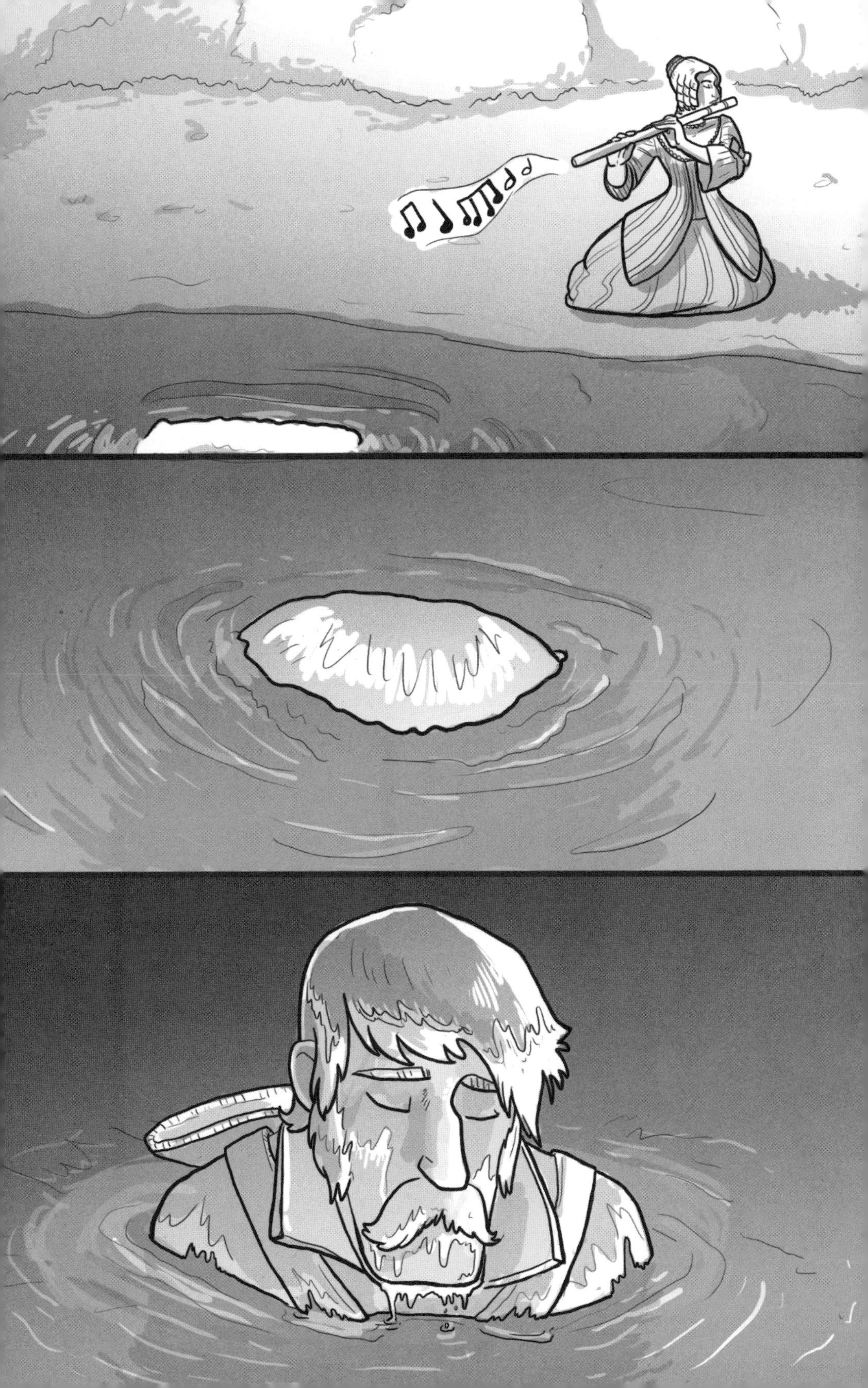

And they lived happily ever after.

BISCLAVRET
STORY
BY MARIE
DE FRANCE
ART
BY KEL
McDONALD

Esme?

Yes milady?

Have you seen my husband?
No, mistress.

Has he disappeared again?
GAHH

Excuse me, your Ladyship.
Sir Robin is here.
Good day Lady Bisclavret.
Good day to you as well, Kind sir.
I came to have audience with your husband.
But alas, he seems to be missing.

Is there anything I could help you with in his stead?
I will return in the evening to see if he has returned.
If he has not, I shall seek your assistance.
You have returned.

I was so very worried.
There was no need. I always return.
Lord, my sweet and tender friend, if I dared, I would like to ask you a question, but I fear nothing more than your anger.
Lady, ask your question.
I will never hide something if you ask me and I know the answer.

Upon my word, I am relieved!
Lord, the days when you leave me, I am very scared.
I'm so sick at heart, and so afraid of losing you that if I fast for comfort, I might die soon.
Tell me where you go, where you are, and where you live.
I fear that you love another woman.
If true, it is a very wrong action.

Lady, in the name of God, have mercy,
If I tell you, I fear your love for me will cease and I will be lost.
Please tell me.
You are a good man and always conduct yourself with dignity.
I could not be blessed with a better husband.
Please tell me.

Lady, I become...
werewolf.
I head to the great forest.
Deep into the woods.
Then I become a wolf.
And I live, hunt, and kill.

And where are your clothes?
Lady, that I do not tell you.
Because if I lost them.
I would not be able to return.
Lord, I love you more than anything.
You have nothing to hide nor doubt me on.

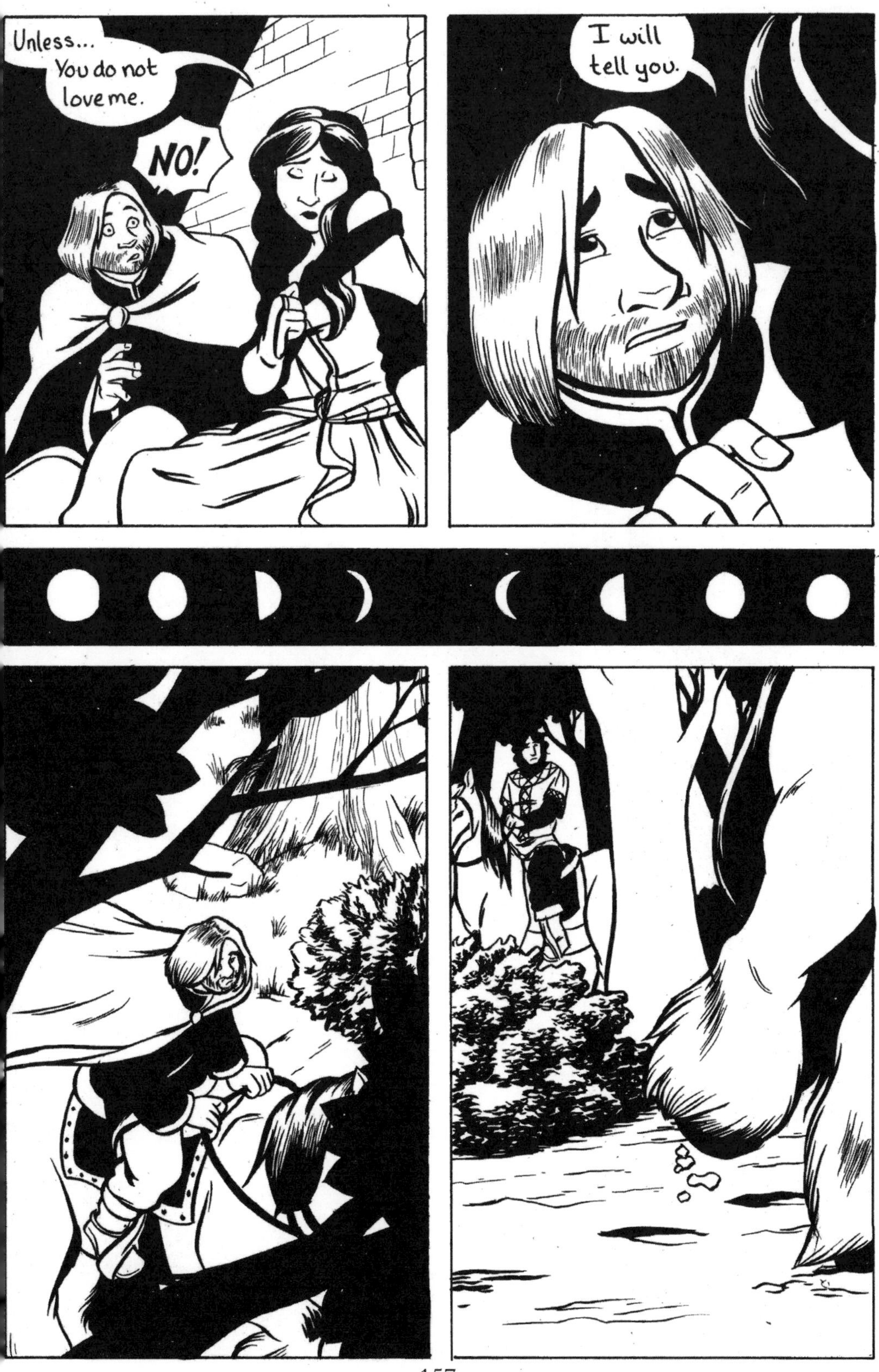
Unless...
You do not
love me.
NO!
I will
tell you.

GAHH
KRK
KRK
KRK
KRK
KRK
POP
KRK
PP
KRK
PP
POP
KP
KEP

AAAOOOOOOO

GRRRR

WOOAFFE

WOOAFFE

There is still no word from Lord Bisclauret?
I always feared he would one day not return.
Fortunately, Sir Robin has made it his duty to protect me.

TMP
TMP
TMP

Whoa, there!
WOOAFFE

Lords, come and see this miracle! Look at how this beast bows!
It has intelligence of a man and implores my pardon.
Gather your dogs.
This beast is endowed with sense and reason, so I give it my protection.

And here is my new pet.
Oh my, how marvelous.
A beast that acts as a gentleman.
Is he tame as well?
He has not once harmed a single member of my court.

GRRRRR

SLAM
ARH

WOAAFFE
GRRR
Lord, I do not understand.
We have all seen and lived with him for several months now.
He has never shown cruelty to anyone before.
Where do you hail for from, Knight?

To what do we owe this honor, Your Highness?
GRRR

K-BING
GRRR

ARGAH
Lady Bisclavret, do you know of any reason why my beast hates you?

And these are the clothes you spoke of?
Yes.

Bring the clothes and my wolf to the next room. Then give it privacy.

We will see if your story is true.

As for you, Madame.
Leave this land and do not return.
While your husband's lands and title are restored to him...
...You are exiled from this country.
LEAVE US NOW!
The end.

Hamelin's Piper
Jose Pimienta

Hamelin
1284

About the Artists

Mary Cagle is the creator of Kiwi Blitz (http://www.kiwiblitz.com), webcomic about a girl, who fights crime with a kiwi mecha. She enjoys blending Eastern and Western styles, and is as passionate about coloring as he is drawing.

C.C. Green wished one day for a big cup of soup and no one gave it to him. o he had to work real hard to get that cup of soup and make it himself. He nade that soup and it was bad. He learned some kind of lesson that day and till wishes for a big cup of soup every now and then, when he isn't really aying attention. You can read his soup at gunshowcomic.com.

Kate Ashwin is a carbon-based life form that lives in Surrey, England. he has two comics, for her sins: Widdershins, which is an ongoing 'ictorianera magical adventure (widdershinscomic.com), and Darken, which is a completed fantasy epic told from the eviller side of things darkencomic.com). Her interests include drawing people in nice coats, rawing people with strange facial expressions, and never drawing a horse nd carriage ever again.

Katie and Steven (Shaggy) Shanahan are comic making siblings who've collaborated on short stories for the Flight anthologies, the web omic Shrub Monkeys, and their own self published comic Silly Kingdom. Katie works as a story board artist for animated tv shows, and Shaggy works n video post production for whatever comes his way. You can catch up with oth of them on their websites (ktshy.com and uberfriendship.com) and ve on ustream every Wednesday at 7:30pm EST on Shanahanigans Live.

Lin Visel a.k.a. **Ovens** works on the comics Effort Comics, Spacy Lucy, Mr. Invisible, and Delicious Confections. If you'd like to contact her, you an at: Chipperwhale@gmail.com

Carla Speed McNeil Carla Speed McNeil is from Louisiana no matter ow long she's lived anywhere else, lives for the flow state in everything he does including re-envisioning fairy tales, has a husband, two kids, four ats, and too many cookbooks, and can't choose a preferred pronoun to ave her life.

Kory Bing was named after a Harry Chapin song that her parents spelle
wrong on purpose. Born three days before Halloween, she grew up in a
isolated river valley in the middle of Missouri, then moved to the Ozarks fc
some reason. Now she lives in Portland with all the other cool kids, makin
Skin Deep, which can be read at www.skindeepcomic.com. You can see he
other art at www.korybing.com.

Kel McDonald draws comics all day, everyday. She she puts all thes
comics on her Sorcery 101 site www.sorcery101.net. She likes to burgers.

Jose Pimienta draws most of the time or is having coffee while listening t
music. He still lives in the U.S. and likes to walk as often as possible to th
beat of a good tune. Most of his comic work is in collaboration with othe
writers and artists such as Lindsay Durbin, Lauren Affe, Jason Franks, Ke
McDonald, and Van Jensen.
www.the-joepi.blogspot.com
www.rawpads.blogspot.com

Extras

One of Lin's first character drawings for Rapunzel and the prince.

Sisters

Left: Katie's concept art for *Tatterhood* featuring the two sisters of the story.

Below: Mary's character design for Jack. She wanted to give him hair that looks like a leaf.

Kory's concept sketches for
The Nixie of the Mill-Pond